Daniel Learns to Swim

Adapted by Alexandra Cassel Schwartz
Based on the screenplay "Daniel's First Swim Class"
written by Alexandra Cassel Schwartz
Poses and layouts by Jason Fruchter

Simon Spotlight
New York London Toronto Sydney New Delhi

SIMON SPOTLIGHT
An imprint of Simon & Schuster Children's Publishing Division
1230 Avenue of the Americas, New York, New York 10020
This Simon Spotlight paperback edition May 2023
© 2023 The Fred Rogers Company
All rights reserved, including the right of reproduction in whole or in part in any form.
SIMON SPOTLIGHT and colophon are registered trademarks of Simon & Schuster, Inc.
For information about special discounts for bulk purchases, please contact Simon & Schuster
Special Sales at 1-866-506-1949 or business@simonandschuster.com.
Manufactured in the United States of America 0323 LAK
10 9 8 7 6 5 4 3 2 1
ISBN 978-1-6659-3326-1
ISBN 978-1-6659-3327-8 (ebook)

It was a very sunny day in the neighborhood, and Daniel Tiger was getting ready to go somewhere special. "I'm wearing my bathing suit and sunscreen," Daniel said. "Can you guess where I'm going?"

"To the neighborhood pool!" Daniel exclaimed. Daniel was going to have his very first swim class.

Daniel saw Prince Tuesday, the lifeguard, sitting in a chair way up high.

"He can see everybody from up there," Mom Tiger explained. "The lifeguard keeps us safe at the pool."

"There are three rules at our neighborhood pool," said Prince Tuesday. "Listen to the lifeguard. No running, because we don't want you to slip and fall. And ask a grown-up if it's okay to go in the water."

Daniel nodded and sang,

♪ ♪ *"Follow the rules to stay safe at the pool!"* ♪ ♪

"You always need a grown-up watching you at the pool," Mom said, "so stay on the bench until your swim teacher is ready for you."

Daniel said "okay" and joined his friends Katerina Kittycat and Miss Elaina as they waited for their swim class to begin.

Daniel saw lots of colorful pool noodles. "I can't wait to use a pool noodle in the water," Daniel said. While they waited, Daniel imagined he was using ALL the pool noodles at a pool noodle party!

Put your sunscreen on and jump on in.
This pool noodle party is about to begin!
'Cause there are noodles, noodles, in the pool.
Noodles, noodles, in the pool.
Bend and wiggle.
We all giggle at our pool noodle party!

Splashing and swimming and having fun,
there's a noodle in the pool for everyone!
'Cause there are noodles, noodles, in the pool.
Noodles, noodles, in the pool.
Bend and wiggle.
We all giggle at our pool noodle party!

"Do you think the water is cold or warm?" Daniel wondered. "I'll go check!"

Luckily, Prince Tuesday, the lifeguard, came quickly and helped Daniel out of the water. He said, "Remember, Daniel, you have to follow the rules to stay safe at the pool."

"But I was only putting my feet in," Daniel said.
"Even if you're just putting your feet in, you could still fall in the water," Prince Tuesday explained, "so you have to ask a grown-up."

It was time for Daniel's swim class to begin. Queen Sara, the swim teacher, led the way to the pool steps, but Daniel was feeling a little nervous to go back in the water.

Daniel took some time to get comfortable.
"Sometimes it helps to watch someone else go first," said Queen Sara.
"You can watch me!" Miss Elaina said. "Whee! It feels like I'm floating!"

Once Daniel saw how much fun Miss Elaina was having in the pool, he felt ready to give it a try too. Daniel liked splish-splashing his legs in the water. He even got to use a pool noodle!

But when Queen Sara asked if he wanted to blow bubbles, Daniel was feeling nervous to put his face in the water.

Daniel remembered that if he followed the rules, he would stay safe at the pool.

"That's right," Queen Sara said. "I'm here, and I'll keep you safe."

Daniel tried blowing bubbles. "I did it! I like blowing bubbles!" Daniel was proud of himself for trying it!

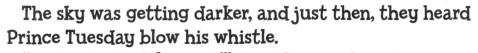

The sky was getting darker, and just then, they heard Prince Tuesday blow his whistle.

"Listen to the lifeguard!" Daniel remembered.

Prince Tuesday told the swimmers to get out of the pool because it wasn't safe to swim if there was a storm.

When the storm clouds passed, the lifeguard blew his whistle. "It's safe to go back in the pool now!"

Daniel cheered. "I really liked swim class. Following the rules helped me stay safe at the pool. Who can YOU ask to go in the water with you? Ugga Mugga!"